ALSO BY BRIAN KEENE

NON-SERIES:

Alone ~ An Occurrence in Crazy Bear Valley ~ The Cage ~ Castaways ~ The Complex ~ The Damned Highway *(with Nick Mamatas)* ~ Darkness on the Edge of Town ~ Dead Sea ~ Dissonant Harmonies *(with Bev Vincent)* ~ Entombed ~ Ghoul ~ The Girl on the Glider ~ Island of the Dead ~ Jack's Magic Beans ~ Kill Whitey ~ Monsters of Saipan *(with Weston Ochse)* ~ Nemesai *(with John Urbancik)* ~ Pressure ~ School's Out ~ Scratch ~ Shades *(with Geoff Cooper)* ~ Silverwood: The Door *(with Richard Chizmar, Stephen Kozeniewski, Michelle Garza and Melissa Lason)* ~ Sixty-Five Stirrup Iron Road *(with Edward Lee, Jack Ketchum, J.F. Gonzalez, Bryan Smith, Wrath James White, Nate Southard, Ryan Harding, and Shane McKenzie)* ~ Take the Long Way Home ~ Tequila's Sunrise ~ Terminal ~ Thor: Metal Gods *(with Aaron Stewart-Ahn, Yoon Ha Lee and Jay Edidin)* ~ White Fire ~ With Teeth

THE RISING SERIES:

The Rising ~ City of the Dead ~ The Rising: Selected Scenes From the End of the World ~ The Rising: Deliverance

THE EARTHWORM GODS SERIES:

Earthworm Gods *(also published as* The Conqueror Worms*)* ~ Earthworm Gods II: Deluge ~ Earthworm Gods: Selected Scenes From the End of the World

THE LEVI STOLTZFUS SERIES:

Dark Hollow ~ Ghost Walk ~ A Gathering of Crows ~ Last of the
Albatwitches ~ Invisible Monsters

THE LABYRINTH SERIES:

The Seven ~ Submerged ~ Splintered

THE CLICKERS SERIES *(with J.F. Gonzalez)*:

Clickers II: The Next Wave ~ Clickers III: Dagon Rising ~ Clickers vs.
Zombies

THE LOST LEVEL SERIES:

The Lost Level ~ Return To the Lost Level ~ Hole In the World ~
Beneath the Lost Level

THE ROGAN SERIES *(with Steven L. Shrewsbury)*:

King of the Bastards ~ Throne of the Bastards ~ Curse of the Bastards

THE GOTHIC SERIES:

Urban Gothic ~ Suburban Gothic *(with Bryan Smith)*

NON-FICTION:

End of the Road ~ The Triangle of Belief ~ Trigger Warnings ~ Unsafe
Spaces ~ Other Words ~ Sundancing ~ Sympathy For the Devil: The
Best of Hail Saten Vol. 1 ~ Running With the Devil: The Best of Hail
Saten Vol. 2 ~ The New Fear: The Best of Hail Saten Vol. 3 ~ Leader of
the Banned: The Best of Hail Saten Vol. 4

COLLECTIONS:

Blood on the Page: The Complete Short Fiction, Vol. 1 ~ All Dark, All the Time: The Complete Short Fiction, Vol. 2 ~ Love Letters From A Nihilist: The Complete Short Fiction, Vol 3 ~ Where We Live and Die ~ A Little Silver Book of Streetwise Stories ~ 4X4 *(with Geoff Cooper, Michael Oliveri, and Michael T. Huyck Jr.)* ~ No Rest For The Wicked ~ No Rest At All ~ Fear of Gravity ~ Unhappy Endings ~ A Conspiracy of One ~ The Cruelty of Autumn ~ Good Things For Bad People ~ A Little Sorrowed Talk ~ Stories For the Next Pandemic ~ Things Left Behind *(with Mary SanGiovanni)*

GRAPHIC NOVELS:

The Last Zombie: Dead New World ~ The Last Zombie: Inferno ~ The Last Zombie: Neverland ~ The Last Zombie: Before the After ~ The Last Zombie: The End ~ Dead of Night: Devil-Slayer ~ He-Man and the Masters of the Universe: Origins of Eternia ~ A Very DC Halloween ~ DC House of Horror ~ Gwendy's Button Box ~ The Fallen

MISCELLANY:

A Field Guide To the Thirteen *(with Mark Sylva)* ~ Apocrypha ~ Liber Nigrum Scientia Secreta *(with J.F. Gonzalez)* ~ Terminal: The Play *(with Roy C. Booth)*

OMNIBUSES:

LeHorn's Hollow ~ The Last Zombie

AS EDITOR:

Clickers Forever: A Tribute to J.F. Gonzalez ~ The Drive-In: Multiplex *(with Christopher Golden)* ~ The Best of Horrorfind ~ The Best of Horrorfind II ~ Operation Ice Bat ~ In Delirium ~ New Dark Visions 2 ~ New Dawn ~ The Daughters of Inanna

ALONE

BRIAN KEENE

For Jack Haringa. One day my semi-colons will rule the planet, and on that day, you shall weep.

ACKNOWLEDGMENTS

Thanks to my pre-readers Mark Sylva and Tod Clark; John Urbancik; Amanda Schuckman; Fredric Brown; Shooter Jennings; Mary SanGiovanni; and my sons.

CONTENTS

"And as imagination bodies forth
The forms of things unknown, the poet's pen
Turns them to shapes and gives to airy nothing..."

William Shakespeare, A Midsummer Night's
    Dream

"These burning skies, dark as a plague of flies, forever
*   and ever and ever together illuminate you and I."*

Shooter Jennings, The Illuminated

1

———

Daniel Miller woke up alone; something he hadn't done since he and Jerry had moved in together after buying this house six years ago.

The first thing he was aware of when he woke each morning was Jerry's presence. Dan could always sense his partner, even without opening his eyes. He could always hear Jerry breathing, smell his scent, feel his weight on the mattress, or the sheets shifting as Jerry stirred. But there was none of that this morning. There was no gentle snoring or faint hint of yesterday's cologne or rustling of their flannel sheets. The bedroom was silent and Jerry was gone. Dan listened for the telltale sounds of his partner making coffee downstairs, or fixing breakfast for Danielle, their adoptive daughter (named after him), or maybe the sound of the shower running, or Jerry bustling around getting ready for work, but there was only more silence.

Yawning, Dan opened his eyes. He rubbed sleep from them, scratched, and yawned again. Something felt... *off*. He lay there for a minute, trying to figure out what it was, and then it dawned on him. The light in the room was different this morning. Gray murk had replaced the usual sunlight that filtered through the closed curtains and blinds. The bedroom was quiet. No, not just quiet. 'Still' seemed a more apt description, Dan thought. It almost felt as if he'd gone deaf. Surely there should have been a noise from somewhere in the house, or from the street? Wondering what time it was, he turned to the nightstand and squinted at the alarm clock.

"Shit."

The digital clock's face was blank. Dan assumed that the power must have gone out sometime in the night. He fumbled for his Rolex watch on the nightstand. It was a gift from Jerry for their fifth anniversary. Although he could have afforded one, Dan would have never purchased such an expensive watch on his own. He accidentally knocked his wallet and keys to the floor in the process of grabbing the watch. The keys made a curiously muted sound as they hit the uncarpeted wood floor. Dan held the watch up and squinted again. The watch had stopped running too; its hands frozen at 1:46 am.

"Keeps on ticking, my ass."

He wondered why he bothered to still rely on the Rolex. His cell phone displayed the time whenever he needed it. The watch was more decorative and sentimental, than anything.

"I don't need you anymore," he said to the Rolex. "The only reason I keep you around is because I'm a softie. Settling down does that to a man, I guess."

Yawning again, he seized the alarm clock again, and shook it, thinking perhaps it had an electrical short. Despite the shaking, the display still didn't light up. All he succeeded in doing was yanking the cord from the outlet.

"Damn it."

Angered, Dan flung the clock across the room and stumbled out of bed. He had a flash of annoyance when the clock hit the wall with a dull thud, rather than the destructive crash he'd been hoping for. With the annoyance came shame that he had acted so thoughtlessly and impulsively. Sure, he was successful now, but he'd grown up poor. Had he really become one of those guys who simply broke things in fits of anger and then went out and bought a replacement? He hoped not. But still — he didn't like being late. Today was going to be a busy one, and this wasn't a good start. And where the hell were Jerry and Danielle?

"Jerry?" His shout was garbled, hoarse. He'd quit smoking three years earlier, after the doctor had warned him about his heart, but the tobacco's effects lingered. He cleared his throat and tried again.

"Hey, Jerry? Hon? The power's out! What time is it?"

There was no answer. His words hung in the air like balloons.

"Jerry?"

Barefoot and clad only in a pair of black, worn-out silk boxer shorts, Dan shuffled into the hall. His ears rang in the silence.

"Helloooooo!"

Dan scratched beneath his waistband and peeked into Danielle's room. The bed was unmade, and the sheets still showed the impression from where she'd slept. His daughter's stuffed animals were silent and dour. Two-dozen glass button eyes stared back at him.

"Danielle? Punkin'?"

No answer.

Dan frowned, thinking. Apparently, Jerry had taken Danielle somewhere this morning. Probably to daycare. He must have known that the power was out. Why hadn't he woken him up before they left? Now he'd be late for work. It was uncharacteristic of Jerry to be so inconsiderate, and it pissed him off the more he thought about it. Sure, Dan was the owner of his own company. But that didn't mean he could just stroll in whenever he felt like it — especially when he only had five other employees, all of whom would be there waiting for him to open.

He thought about the possibilities. Danielle was late for daycare and Jerry had forgotten about waking him. Or perhaps the power had gone off after Jerry and Danielle had left the house. Or maybe something terrible had happened, and Jerry had to rush her to the doctor. Or maybe Jerry had left him — moved out while he was still asleep. Maybe he'd been having an affair with another guy...

Quit being paranoid. Jerry probably just went out for something —maybe we need coffee — and he left a note downstairs.

Dan stomped down the hallway and into the bathroom. He assured himself that he was just being silly and paranoid. He needed to wake up. Then everything would become clear.

He wished, not for the first time, that they'd bought a newer house with room for a second bathroom. Instead, they'd bought this Civil War-era home with limited space. Still, it was a home filled with love and laughter — except for this morning.

Fumbling for his limp penis through the fly of his boxers, he thought about this new sign of approaching middle age. Gone was the raging morning wood of his twenties and early thirties. He stared down at his potbelly, another sign, one that had come to visit him around his thirty-second birthday, and refused to leave no matter how much time he spent at the gym or how much healthy food Jerry forced him to eat.

He stood there, willing himself to piss, but nothing happened. He concentrated, focusing on the act at hand — or in hand. Still nothing. His penis had stage fright. The first few gray pubic hairs (another unwelcome and disturbing sign of impending middle-age, one that had shown up only a few months ago) poked out from his boxers. More gray peppered his temples and beard. Dan hated the gray hairs. Jerry often told him they were sexy, and that they made him look distinguished, but Dan knew he was lying. It was one of those things you said out of love, rather than sincerity — like telling someone a particular pair of jeans didn't make them look fat when in fact, they did.

Muttering, Dan released his flaccid, uncooperative member and shuffled back to the bedroom. He shrugged into his blue bathrobe, mildly surprised that his joints didn't pop and his muscles didn't ache this morning like they usually did. That was a good sign.

The silence began to annoy him. It felt uncomfortable. Yawning once again, he grabbed the stereo remote control and pushed the button. Nothing happened. Then Dan remembered that there was no electricity.

"Must... have... coffee... Can't think straight."

He fastened the bathrobe shut, and started down the stairs, mentally taking stock as he went.

My name is Daniel Miller. I own a web design and hosting company that helped pay for this house. I have a wonderful partner, Jerry, who works as a mortgage research analyst, and a beautiful daughter, Danielle, and I love them both very much, even if they did forget to wake me up for work this morning. I am officially middle aged now, and somebody must have made a mistake somewhere, because I graduated in 1990, which wasn't really that long ago, and I've already got a pot belly and gray fucking pubic hair and no morning hard on. This makes me angry. The power is out, and this makes me even angrier. And even if the power was on, the classic rock station out of Harrisburg is playing Def Leppard and Bon Jovi these days. When did Def fucking Leppard become classic rock anyway? Classic rock is Jimi Hendrix and Led Zeppelin. And Bon Jovi? That was what straight guys listened to when they wanted to get laid back in the Eighties. It certainly isn't something I want to wake up to in the morning.

"Hello," he called again as he entered the living room, not really expecting a response. "Anybody home? Come out, come out wherever you are."

He made his way into the kitchen, and looked for a note on the refrigerator, but found none. The appliance was covered with the same old magnets and take-out menus. Hanging from the center of the door was a crayon drawing Danielle had made of the three of them. He'd hung it up there only a few weeks ago, and the three of them had decorated it with gold stars and glitter. Sighing, Dan opened the cupboard, and noticed that the hinges on the cupboard door didn't squeak like normal.

Jerry must have oiled them yesterday. Probably got sick of waiting for me to do it. But that's not my fault. He knows how busy I've been with work.

Dan pulled out a jar of instant coffee, and dropped two spoonfuls into a mug. He hated how instant coffee tasted, but with no power, he had little choice. Then he turned on the hot water tap. Nothing happened.

"Oh, for crying out loud! There's no water either?"

He slammed the mug down on the counter. The noise was quiet, muted, and not at all satisfying, so he slammed it down again. It still wasn't loud enough to express his anger. The mug didn't rattle or crack. The impact seemed suppressed, as if both the counter and the mug were made of rubber. It occurred to him that his alarm clock had made a similar sound when he'd tossed it across the bedroom minutes before. Dan stuck the tip of his pinky finger in each ear and wiggled it around, thinking that perhaps his ears were plugged. The sensation felt good, but when he pulled his finger out and examined it, there was very little wax, and his hearing hadn't changed.

Shrugging, Dan decided to call time and temperature, find out how late he was, and then call the power and water companies before he left for work. Luckily, the kitchen phone wasn't a cordless, and it didn't need electricity to work. He lifted the phone from its cradle and brought it to his ear. All he heard was more silence. Dan toyed with it, trying to get a dial tone, but to no avail. The phone slipped from his hand, and tumbled to the floor without a sound. The first twinge of unease gnawed at him. The dead utilities and his missing family... What the hell was going on? Had there been an accident or something? A terrorist attack? No, he was just being silly. There had to be a logical explanation. He just needed to wake up. Then things would make sense.

He opened the refrigerator and pulled out a carton of orange juice. Still pondering the situation, he brought the carton to his lips, drank, grimaced, and then spit the juice out in the sink. It had no taste. It wasn't rancid. It was just —*tasteless*. The milk and soda had the same effect when he tried them. Even the bottled water tasted strange — flat. He grabbed a cold chicken drumstick, and took a bite.

"Ugh!"

Disgusted, he threw it into the garbage can. The chicken was also tasteless. Like chewing on a piece of paper. Could the stuff in the fridge have gone bad already? Just how long had the power been out? How long had he been asleep? And for that matter, where had the chicken come from? As far as Dan remembered, they'd had lasagna last night. Where were those leftovers?

"Jerry?" He called out again, not expecting an answer. "Danielle? Are you guys here?"

No response.

Sighing, he tightened the belt of his robe and decided to get the newspaper. Maybe there had been a thunderstorm overnight, and he'd slept through it. Maybe it had knocked down the power lines or something. That would explain the utility outage, at the very least.

Dan walked to the front door, his bare feet swishing on the carpet. Normally the sound was very loud, but this morning, it too seemed quieter. He wondered again about his ears. Was there something wrong with his hearing? First sign of an oncoming sinus infection, perhaps?

He opened the door, stepped onto the sidewalk, and noticed that the light outside was different, as well. He stared up at the dark and overcast sky. It looked strange. There was no sun, and no clouds. Instead, there was only a bleak, gray curtain. It didn't billow. Didn't move. He'd never seen anything like it before. The haze was like fog, but seemed... denser, somehow. Too thick. It obscured everything. He could see a few of his neighbor's houses — the Kresby's and the Lopez's—in each direction, and some of the trees lining the street, but after that there was nothing but more gray haze. Dan frowned. It was as if the rest of the neighborhood had been swallowed up by the weird fog.

He was annoyed to discover that the newspaper wasn't on the sidewalk. The delivery boy was usually pretty good about throwing it there. The kid had an arm like a major league player and the precision of an Army sniper. Dan took a few more steps, searching for the paper. Then he looked at the driveway — and froze.

"Oh no..."

Jerry's silver Lexus was still in the driveway, parked in front of Dan's brand new Ford Explorer.

Tiny pangs of real fear blossomed inside of him now, replacing his anger. He stood there, his pulse quickening as panic set in. Where the hell was his family? Could Danielle have been abducted, like other children in the news? Kidnapped — and Jerry killed, trying to protect her? Or a hate crime, perhaps? Maybe some sick fuck had them right now! His partner and daughter could be out there, and—

He punched his leg in frustration as a new thought occurred to him.

"The cell phone! Why didn't I think of that before?"

Because you just woke up, moron.

Dan ran back into the house, through the kitchen and living room, and took the stairs three at a time. Yes, the kitchen phone hadn't worked, but it relied on the physical phone lines. That didn't necessarily mean the cellular network was down. Rushing into the bedroom, he grabbed the cell phone from its charger on the nightstand and pressed the power button, turning it on. Even with the power outage, the battery should have still had plenty of life.

Except that it didn't. The cell phone sat silently in his hands. He waited for it to power up, but it didn't. The screen stayed blank and dim.

"Come on!"

Dan thumbed the power button again, and then, without waiting for the screen to light up, he dialed 911. Again there was nothing. The cell phone, like everything else in the house, was dead.

"I don't believe this..."

Standing there in his bathrobe, Dan suddenly felt weak. He thought he might pass out. His head swooned and his vision darkened. His loved ones were missing, and something strange was going on. His stomach felt sick. Dan dropped the cell phone and sank onto the bed, clutching the sheets with his fists, and trying to keep his growing fear from overwhelming him.

He didn't even notice that the mattress springs did not squeak.

2

He sat there a few moments, trembling, his head throbbing, not from pain, but from terror. The fear and nausea grew stronger, and his stomach cramped. Dan slapped a hand over his mouth and ran to the bathroom. He knelt and gagged, but nothing came out. Desperate for relief, he stuck his middle finger down his throat and tried forcing himself to vomit. It didn't help. Nothing came out but air.

Standing back up, Dan cinched his robe around him and tried to think. Something was terribly wrong, that much was obvious. He needed to call the police. If something sinister really had happened to Jerry and Danielle, then every second mattered. But he couldn't report it as long as the power was out and his cell phone wasn't working. He decided to try the Lopez's next door. Maybe their power was on. If not, then maybe their cell phones were working.

He walked back outside again. His apprehension grew as he passed by Jerry's car. Much like his home, the rest of the neighborhood was silent. The typical summer morning sounds were missing. There were no birds chirping from the trees and power lines. The leaves on the trees weren't rustling in the breeze, and no squirrels scampered across them. There were no lawnmowers roaring to life. No children playing and shouting in their yards. No traffic in the street. No booming car stereos as the teenagers cruised by—no cruising teenagers either.

Dan stared upward into the gray sky. No planes passed overhead, even though they lived just a few miles from the airport. There weren't even any contrails from airplanes that had already passed by. It was possible that the murky, overcast haze obscured them, but at the very least, he would have still been able to hear the planes overhead. They were a regular occurrence. But not this morning, and that meant trouble. The last time the planes were absent from the sky was the day after September 11th, when the President had shut down all air traffic in the country.

Dan's dread grew. He stepped onto his neighbor's lawn. The grass should have been wet with morning dew, but it was curiously dry and brittle. The leaves drooped on the trees.

You really need to water your yard, Hector, he thought.

The Lopez family had moved onto the block the same year as Dan and Jerry, and they'd grown close over time. Hector Lopez, his wife Estelle, and his teenage daughter Maria, were good people, and had no problem with a gay couple living next door — let alone a gay couple raising an adoptive daughter. Hector had mentioned once that Maria suffered from depression. She had apparently gone through a self-mutilation phase, cutting herself with knives, but all that had changed now that they'd moved here. Dan liked the family very much.

Hector commuted into the city every morning, and Estelle worked part-time at the mall. When Dan peeked through their garage door window, he saw that both Hector and Estelle's cars were still inside. Maria's sporty little Volkswagen, purchased for her several months ago as a sweet-sixteen present, sat in the driveway. Dan felt a rush of relief. All three of them were obviously home. Sitting next to the vehicles was the new bass boat Hector had purchased only a few weeks before.

Dan crept up the sidewalk, suddenly aware that he was parading around in his bathrobe. But so what? Why should he care what anyone thought right now? This was no time to feel self-conscious. Jerry and Danielle were gone, and they were all that mattered. He rang the doorbell. The chime didn't sound and the button didn't light up. He rang it again, hopeful, but nothing happened.

"The power must be out here, too."

He knocked, instead, and waited. When there was no answer, Dan knocked again, listening carefully for sounds from inside the house. He was greeted by silence. Cursing, he rapped again, harder this time. Nothing. He beat the door with both fists, hammering on it, hollering for Hector and Estelle and Maria — shouting for somebody, anybody, to help him. Even in his panic, Dan was aware once again of the curious, muted sound effect. The door shook in its frame, yet his blows were muffled. Even his cries sounded small in the silence. He didn't have time to ponder it now. He reached down and tried the doorknob. It was locked. He rattled it, then slammed the door with his shoulder. His efforts produced nothing.

Moaning, he ran back to his yard and cut across it to the Kresby's house. Their grass also felt dry and withered.

Jesus, doesn't anybody take care of their lawn anymore?

His robe had come unfastened and it flapped behind him, fluttering like a cape. If any of the neighbors were watching him right now, he realized, they were getting quite the show.

I probably look like a middle-aged superhero, he thought. *Fuck them. If they don't like it, they can close the shades.*

It occurred to him that other than the Kresby's and the Lopez's, nobody could see him anyway. The gray fog obliterated everything else. He could see the road and a few of the homes across the street, and the cars in their driveways, but beyond that was emptiness. Indeed, the neighborhood just sort of faded away, vanishing into the murk. Chances were he could run around naked out here and no one would know. He almost wished somebody *could* see him. If ripping off his robe and boxers and letting his dick flap in the breeze would make someone call the police, he'd be all for it.

Focus, he thought. *You're freaking out, and that's not going to help Jerry or Danielle. Get a grip on yourself. The Kresby's will be home. They're retired. They never go anywhere, except to the grocery store on Friday. Phil's prostate wakes him up early every morning. He'll answer. He'll help.*

Except that Phil Kresby didn't answer the door. Neither did his wife, Susan. Dan's urgent knocks and cries for help went unanswered, just as they had at the Lopez home. Frantic, he pressed his face against the Kresby's large bay window at the front of the house. The curtains were slightly parted. Dan cupped his hands beside his eyes and peered through the glass. It was hard to see more than a few feet inside. The Kresby's living room was filled with the same gray fog that obscured the rest of the neighborhood.

"What the hell is going on? What is this?"

Dan realized that his voice sounded very strange out here in the silence. He had trouble believing it was he who had spoken aloud. He scowled, wondering how the fog had gotten inside the Kresby's home. Had they left a window open or something? Were they okay? Could something have happened to them, too?

"Phil," he shouted, banging on the window and noticing the strange muffling effect again. "Phil? Susan? Are you home? It's Dan Miller! Please, if you're in there, answer me. I need help. Something has happened."

Dan glanced around the yard, spotted a ceramic lawn gnome squatting between two of the Kresby's bushes, and picked it up. He noticed that the shrubs had the same withered look and texture as the grass and trees, but then he turned his attention to the gnome. It was solid, but surprisingly light. Dan smashed the lawn ornament's pointed green hat against the window. The glass shattered on the third blow. For a brief second, Dan thought he heard a woman scream, as if from a far off distance, but then the sound faded. Shards of glass fell quietly at his feet. Again, he wondered what was going on with his hearing. The sound of breaking glass should have been much louder. And who had he heard screaming? Had it been Susan? If so, she must be upstairs, given how far away she'd sounded.

"Susan? Are you in there? I'm sorry about the window, but I need help."

He paused, listening, but there was no response. Yet he couldn't have imagined the scream, could he? There had to be someone here.

"Susan! Answer me, god damn it! Something very strange is going on. I'm coming in. I don't mean any harm. If you're in there, let me know."

When he still didn't receive a response, Dan carefully picked the shards of glass out of the frame and then climbed through the broken window. He watched where he stepped on the other side, mindful of his bare feet. Once inside the Kresby's home, he was immediately overcome by a vague sense of unease. At first, he chalked it up to the situation — his family was missing and he had just broken into his neighbor's house. But as he crept forward into the living room, that feeling of dread increased. Something was wrong in here. He didn't know what it was. He couldn't name it or define it or explain the cause. He just felt it on some instinctive level.

The gloom deepened as he went further, obscuring his vision. Hesitating, Dan reached out and tried to touch the gray haze, but his hand simply passed through it as if it weren't there. He thought back to an experience he'd had when he and

Jerry first started dating. They'd gone mountain climbing together for a weekend, and at the top of a peak, he'd touched the low-hanging mist. At the time, Jerry had made a joke of it, saying that his love for Dan made him feel like he was walking amidst the clouds. Dan remembered the sensation as he'd waved his hand through the fog in the Kresby's home. This wasn't the same as on the mountain. There was no sense of dampness or cold. Indeed, the grayness felt like nothing at all. It had no temperature or texture or smell. He stepped into it, and that sense of foreboding increased.

"Phil?" he called again, but now his voice had grown timid. "Susan? Please answer me. Please...?"

His feet faltered in time with his voice. The unreasonable fear deepened, threatening to overwhelm him. The deeper he went into the fog, the worse the feeling became. Dan still had no idea just what he was afraid of. He only knew that he had to get out of the house. Turning, he fled across the room, heedless of the broken glass, and hurried back out the window. His unease subsided as he left the gray haze behind, and his worries for Jerry and Danielle returned to the forefront again.

Seized with panic for his family, Dan charged across his neighbor's yard, dodged around a tree, and ran out into the street. He shouted as loudly as he could, but his cries sounded hollow and meek. He half wondered if the strange atmosphere was having some kind of dampening effect on sound. He plunged through more of the gloom as he ran across the street. The pavement beneath his feet vanished. He glanced around, looking for the houses and trees that he knew were there, but saw only a wall of gray. Even the curb was gone.

Plow through, he thought. *It's just fog. A weird fucking fog, but fog all the same. You can do this. You need to find out what's happened.*

Trying hard to ignore his fears, he forced himself to continue ahead. As he did, the nameless dread returned again, growing stronger with each subsequent step. He kept going, realizing that he was well past where the curb should have been. Despite this, there was no grass beneath his feet. No yard. No houses or trees or trash cans or mailboxes. It was as if everything on the block, other than his home and the Lopez and Kresby homes had vanished. He turned to look behind him and saw his own house. It seemed to be shimmering. The image made Dan think of the way heat waves were sometimes visible rising off a hot road surface. He took a deep breath, trying to clear his head and make sense of things, and that was when he felt it.

Someone — or some *thing* — was here with him, inside the fog. He couldn't see them or hear them, but he definitely felt a presence.

"H-hello?"

He saw no movement, but he sensed it all the same. Something was coming toward him, pushing its way through the haze. His dread increased. The disembodied presence drew closer. He still couldn't see it, but the grayness seemed to press around him.

"Who's there?"

For a second, the gloom parted, and Dan caught a glimpse of a looming, shadowy figure. It wasn't human. That much he was sure of. He saw no distinguishing features or traits. No face or clothing. The entity seemed to be nothing more than a black, man-shaped hole, but much larger than a human. It towered over him, dwarfing him with its presence. The grayness seemed to congeal in the figure's wake. Dan felt the creatures eyes upon him, even though he couldn't see any. Then, the shadow reached for him.

Screaming, Dan fled back across the street. He ran across his yard and into his house, slamming the door behind him. His fingers trembled so badly that he had trouble working the deadbolt. When the door was locked, he sank to the floor and bit his fist to keep from shrieking.

Dan had no idea how long he crouched there with his back against the door, shivering, stifling his gasps and moans. Slowly, his fear subsided. He listened carefully, but if the shadow had pursued him, then it made no sound. Eventually, he gathered enough courage to crawl over to the window. Then he peeked outside. The yard and street were empty. If the thing was still out there, then it was hiding in the haze.

Trying to be as quiet as possible, Dan went from room to room and repeated the process. He peered out each window, looking for any sign of his pursuer. He made sure all the doors and windows were locked. Satisfied that he wasn't in any immediate danger, he collapsed into a dining room chair, buried his face in his hands. He wanted to weep, but the tears, like his urine earlier that morning, refused to flow.

3

———————

Dan gripped the pen so tightly between his thumb and index finger that the plastic casing cracked. Black ink smudged his skin, but he didn't notice. Instead, he kept singing under his breath.

"I'm making a list, and checking it twice. Gonna find out..."

His voice faltered as another sob welled up inside of him. He wanted to cry so bad, but for some reason, he couldn't. Blinking, Dan took a deep breath and forced himself to focus. Then he turned his attention back to the paper lying in front of him on the dining room table. At the top of the paper, in big block capital letters, he'd written THINGS THAT I KNOW. Beneath that was a bullet-point list of all the weird occurrences he'd experienced since waking up this morning.

- Jerry and Danielle are gone.
- Jerry's car is still in the driveway.
- My watch stopped at 1:46 in the morning. It's not working.
- All of the utilities are out.

- Cell phone won't power up. I'm betting even if it did, the coverage isn't working, either.
- The Lopez and Kresby houses seem to be deserted.
- Something is wrong with the sound of things.
- Everything tastes funny. That could be me, I guess. Maybe my hearing and sense of taste are both off.
- There's a gray sort of haze everywhere, but it doesn't feel like fog.
- Everything in the haze seems to have disappeared, including the rest of the neighborhood.
- The plants outside feel weird, like they are dying. Could that be because of the haze?
- The light is different, both indoors and out. It's gray. That's probably also because of the haze, since it's gray, too.
- At one point, my house was shimmering. When I came out of the haze, it stopped.
- There is something else out there in the haze. I'm terrified of it.
- Other than the figure in the mist, I am alone.

WHEN HE WAS FINISHED with the list, Dan leaned back in his chair and sighed. Writing everything down had given him a sense of achievement. It had made him feel like he was doing something useful, and had calmed him somewhat, but he was still scared and worried about his family — and everyone else in the neighborhood, for that matter. He and Jerry had an annual New Year's Eve tradition. Each year, they stayed up late and watched The Twilight Zone marathon on television. Dan's favorite episode had always been the one with the meek and bookish bank teller who is the only survivor of a nuclear war. After everyone else on the planet is dead, the teller is overjoyed that he'll finally have time to read his beloved books without interruption. Dan had always found the premise an enjoyable fantasy, but he regretted that now. There was nothing enjoyable about his predicament.

He took another deep breath and pondered what to do next. He decided to begin by searching the home for clues. He'd been half awake and panicked before. Perhaps if he went back through the house now and searched meticulously, he'd find something that might explain what had happened.

Nodding, Dan went upstairs and returned to the bedroom, intent on retracing his steps. He found Jerry's keys, wallet, and cell phone lying atop the dresser, exactly where Jerry always put them every night. On a whim, he tried Jerry's cell phone, but it was dead just like his. He flipped open the leather wallet. It had belonged to Jerry's grandfather, and had sentimental value. Jerry never left home without it, and was very careful about not losing it. If he had left in the night, Dan was certain that Jerry would have taken the wallet with him. Inside the wallet was forty dollars in cash, along with all of Jerry's credit cards, driver's license, and social security card. There were no pictures. Jerry kept those on his cell phone.

Dan put the wallet back down and noticed that he'd left an ink fingerprint on it. He wiped his smudged fingers on his robe, but only succeeded in smearing the ink more. He shook his head in frustration. With the water off, he couldn't even wash his hands properly.

He opened the dresser drawers. All of Jerry's underwear, socks, ties and t-shirts seemed to be accounted for. The ties made him smile. Unlike most men, Jerry had always insisted on storing his ties in the dresser. Dan had teased him playfully about it many times. He tried the closet, and found Jerry's slacks, jeans, dress shirts, and suit coats hanging in place, many of them covered in the plastic from the dry cleaner's. Jerry's shoes were lined up neatly on the shelf above. Dan counted them. Two pairs of sneakers, a pair of sandals, three pair of dress shoes, and a ratty pair of skateboarding shoes from Jerry's teenage skate punk years that he refused to throw away. Only one pair was missing — Jerry's bedroom slippers. When Dan turned, he saw them sticking out from under the bed.

Okay, he thought. *If Jerry had decided to leave me for some unknown reason, then he would have taken his wallet and his keys. At the very least, he wouldn't have gone barefoot.*

"Where are you?" he asked the room. "Where did you go? What's happened to you?"

He blinked his eyes again, willing them to water, demanding they release the sorrow he felt inside, but they refused. His stomach roiled. He forced himself to calm down, reminded himself to focus again on the task at hand. He couldn't help Jerry or Danielle if he freaked out. He had to stay strong and in control, and approach this illogical situation in a logical manner.

Dan walked down the hall to his daughter's room. It was as it had been when he first woke up. The bed was still unmade, and the sheets still showed the impression of her body from where she'd slept. He wondered about that. How much time had passed since he'd first found himself alone? Without her body weight, wouldn't the sheets and pillow smooth out eventually? He wasn't sure. Although it was Dan who usually tucked Danielle in at night, Jerry was the one who got up with her most mornings.

Where was she? Where was his little girl? Where was the brave, funny, loving child, and why did her room feel so empty? He thought of all the times he had taken Danielle to the airport. It was their special thing to do together. They went there at least twice a week, parking in a small field next to the fenced off runway. Dan would spread a blanket and they would sit in the grass together, eating lunch, and watching the planes land and take off. Seeing the wonder, joy, and excitement in

Danielle's eyes every time a plane passed over filled Dan with happiness.

Now, the memory filled him with dread, because he wondered if they'd ever be able to do that again.

He approached the bed slowly, and forgetting about the ink on his hands, picked up Danielle's pillow and brought it to his face. He breathed deeply, hoping for just a hint of her scent — baby shampoo and hair — but there was nothing. His baby's smell existed only in his memory now. A single blond hair was stuck to the pillowcase. Dan stroked the pillow reverently, and when he closed his eyes, he could see her lying there, sound asleep, and hear her breathing softly. When Danielle was younger, he used to creep into her room late at night and put his hand on her back, just to make sure she was still breathing. Jerry used to laugh about it, reminding him that the baby monitors worked fine, but Dan had never trusted those things. Sometimes, he just liked to be sure. It was comforting to feel her chest moving up and down. Comforting to know that she was safe and sound and secure.

"Daddy?"

His eyes snapped open, and the pillow slipped from his hands. Dan spun around, but the room was empty.

"Danielle? DANIELLE!"

He ran out of the bedroom and into the hall, shouting her name, but the corridor was deserted and he was still alone. It occurred to him that his cries should be echoing in the empty hall, but instead, they sounded flat and meek. The strange dampening effect on sound was still persisting.

"Danielle," he called again, just to be sure she wasn't hiding somewhere. When there was still no answer, he returned to her room and stood in the doorway, staring at her stuffed animals and toys. After a moment, he stepped into the room again and picked up Danielle's favorite, a large pink bunny that they'd bought at Walmart last Easter. Danielle rarely left home without it.

"I imagined it," he told the stuffed rabbit. "I'm just so scared. I miss her. I guess you miss her, too. But don't worry. We'll find her. We'll figure out what's going on."

A quick search of Danielle's closet and dresser confirmed that none of her clothes were missing, either. Dan tried to remember what pajamas he'd dressed her in the night before, after her bath, but couldn't. He realized that he was still holding the stuffed animal in one hand.

"She wouldn't have left you behind. If they had gone some-where, she'd have wanted to take you with her."

He tossed the rabbit back on the bed and wondered what its presence here meant. On the one hand, it could be a good thing. If all of Jerry and Danielle's things were still here, then it meant they hadn't abandoned him or fled in the night — not that Dan could imagine them doing such a thing. Why would they? The three of them had a happy home life here. They were a family. It was inconceivable that Jerry would abscond with their daughter in the middle of the night. But the alternative — that something dire had happened to them—seemed just as perplexing. There were no signs of trauma. No signs of a strug-gle. Indeed, the only signs of violence he'd seen since waking up were the ones he himself had caused—the watch thrown against the wall, and of course, the Kresby's big bay window, shattered with a ceramic lawn gnome. Could there be a logical explanation for everything that was going on? Dan sat down on Danielle's bed and considered this. Yes, there was one possibility.

He was dreaming. He was still asleep in his bed and this was all just one big lucid dream. Or perhaps the term lucid nightmare might be more apt. He glanced around the room, studying everything. It all seemed so real, and his mind seemed so sharp. There was none of the ethereal fuzziness that dreams usually had, although it occurred to him that the gray fog outside most certainly had that quality about it. Other than that, everything else seemed permanent. He felt things when he touched them — their weight and textures. He splayed his ink-stained fingers apart, feeling their stickiness. But his sense of smell, taste and his hearing were both off, just like in a dream. You couldn't smell or taste things in dreams, could you? He didn't think so. He didn't remember ever having done so before. But then again, Dan was fairly certain that you couldn't feel things in dreams, either.

So, what the hell was going on? Was he dreaming, and if so, how much longer would it go on? If he wasn't, then where was everybody? What had happened to them? It was terrifying enough that Jerry and Danielle were missing, but where were his neighbors? More disturbing, who *else* might be missing? How far did this situation extend? Just how alone was he, really?

"I'm dreaming," he said. His voice sounded small in the silence. "I have to be dreaming. It's the only explanation that makes any sense. This is all a dream. Either that..."

He couldn't finish the sentence aloud.

Either that... or I'm going crazy.

Dan looked around his daughter's room again. Each toy or book or piece of clothing was a memory. His stomach roiled again, as a new bout of fear and dismay gripped him.

"Where are you?" he moaned. "What has happened to you? What is happening to me?"

"Daddy?"

Dan raised his head and saw his daughter standing in the doorway looking at him.

"Danielle?"

"Daddy! Are you here?"

As Dan leaped up from the bed, he noticed that Danielle's voice didn't match her lips. Watching her speak was like watching an English-dubbed foreign film. Her lips moved, forming the words just slightly ahead of the sounds.

"Yes, baby." Dan rushed toward her. "I'm here. Daddy's here. I've been so worried about you. Where have you been?"

"Daddy, I'm scared."

"It's okay, pumpkin. I'm here now. It's all going to be—"

He reached for her, intending to sweep Danielle off her feet and hug her tightly to him, reassuring both his daughter and himself that things would be okay (because Dan had noticed over time that one of the odd things about being a parent was when his child skinned her knee or bumped her head, giving her comfort gave him comfort, as well). Instead of pulling her close, his arms went right through Danielle, as if she were composed of smoke. Dan cried out in surprise. His momentum carried him into the bedroom wall, which he bounced off of. Dan tumbled backward and landed on the carpet with his rump. When he looked around, Danielle was gone again.

He sat there for a moment, stunned.

"Danielle? Danielle, come back!"

She didn't. He was alone again. Moaning, he curled into a ball and trembled.

"No. No no no no no…"

The noise started as a whimper, deep down inside of him, before spewing out as a long, breathless shriek.

Dan wasn't sure how much time passed — how long he remained there on his daughter's bedroom floor, curled into the fetal position and screaming with each new breath. His voice didn't turn hoarse and his throat wasn't sore, nor did his tailbone hurt from his fall. He supposed that was because he was numb from shock. The pain would probably catch up with him soon enough. He hoped so, at least. He looked forward to it, because feeling pain would take his mind off feeling scared and helpless, if only for a little while.

Eventually, he found himself downstairs again, seated at the kitchen table. The pad and the paper were where he'd left them, and his notes were still there. Shaking his head, he stared at them. The list was bullshit. In the aftermath of what he'd just witnessed, his options were narrowing. Either he was crazy — which seemed more and more likely — or this was indeed some bizarre dream from which he couldn't awake. Maybe Jerry was still lying next to him, and would wake up any moment, notice that Dan was having some kind of nightmare, and would wake him.

He took a deep breath and waited for it to happen.

Any moment now.

Any moment...

4

He waited for a very long time, but nobody came to wake him.

5

———————

Dan sat there at the table, staring at the wall and not seeing it. Danielle did not appear again. The silence continued, uninterrupted. The light outside didn't change. The grayness remained. So did his fears and sorrow. But while the haze was permanent and unyielding, his emotions were not. They came intermittently, buoyed on waves of numbness. One moment, he felt numb inside. Then, he would think of Jerry or Danielle and the emotions would rush back in. He wished that he could cry. He thought he might feel better if only he could cry. After a while, he realized that he was humming aloud to himself. The song was tuneless.

With a speed that belied his apathy, Dan pushed himself back from the table, knocking the chair to the floor. He leaped to his feet, screaming obscenities. Snatching the pad of paper from the tabletop, he tore his checklist off and crumpled it in his fist. Then he flung the wadded ball across the room. Still shouting, he rampaged through the kitchen, knocking pots and pans from their hooks above the glass-topped oven and pushing the microwave off its cart. The unit gouged and scratched the floor tiles before breaking. Its cord still dangled from the outlet like a disembodied appendage. Dan ripped the silverware drawer from its hinges and tossed it across the room. Then he did the same with the other drawers, spilling their contents into a heap. His rage carried him into the living room, where he kicked over the coffee table and snatched the cushions from the sofa. He punched a hole in the closet door, and then, unsatisfied, he punched it again. He gripped the knob and wrenched the door from its frame, leaving it hanging by only the upper hinge. Then he charged inside the closet and tossed items haphazardly — umbrellas and winter coats and shoes they hadn't worn in years.

Emerging from the closet, he paused again, looking for something else to unleash his frustration upon. Grunting, he pushed the fifty-two inch plasma television off of its stand. Then he jumped up and down on it, grinning as it cracked beneath his heels.

"Jerry! Danielle! Come back. Somebody come and wake me up!"

Still shouting, he grabbed pictures from the wall. He put his foot through a Monet print, his knee through an original canvas painted by a family friend, and then moved on to a set of family photos. Only then did Dan pause. Chest heaving, he stared down at Jerry and Danielle. They stared back up at him, smiling.

"WHERE ARE THEY?" He flung the framed photograph across the room. It slammed into the wall, shattering the glass. Shards rained down on the carpet.

"Bring them back," he yelled. "God damn you God! You bring my family back right now. Right fucking now!"

If God heard him, then He too was silent. Dan glanced around at the wreckage. The tempest had occurred quietly—the sounds of destruction muted just like earlier.

"It's not enough," he moaned. "Make some noise, god damn it."

Panting, he ran to the door and dashed outside.

"Hello," he screamed. "Hello, I'm here! I'm right here. It's me, Daniel Miller. Is there anybody here? Is there anybody left? Can anybody hear me? Please, if you can hear me, say something. Hello? Somebody? Anyone?"

His momentum carried him through the yard and out into the street. Dan stumbled over the curb, but regained his balance. Arms flailing, he fled toward another neighbor's house. Unlike the Lopez or Kresby families, he didn't know this neighbor's name. His interactions with them were limited to nodding at the husband and occasionally waving at the wife. They were an older couple, and kept to themselves. Jerry had always claimed it was because the two were uncomfortable with a gay couple living next door, let alone a gay couple with an adopted child. But Dan had never gotten that vibe from them. They weren't rude. They were just private. Right now, none of that mattered. They could be members of the Westboro Baptist Church for all Dan cared. He'd still be happy to see them. Hell, he'd march right alongside them, lifting his 'God Hates Fags' protest sign high for all to see, if only they answered their door.

Between him and their door, however, was the fog.

He stared at their house, and then turned reluctantly back to his. Dan gasped. His panic and rage dissipated. Seeing Jerry's silver Lexus parked in front of his Ford Explorer made him realize he hadn't tried the cars.

"I can just drive to the police station. Barrel right through this fog. That thing can't get me inside a car. I can drive faster than it can run, can't I?

The silence made him shiver. Dan hurried back to the house and retrieved Jerry's keys. Then he returned to his driveway. Of the two vehicles, he would have preferred his, but Jerry had him parked in. He pointed the remote at the Lexus and thumbed the remote control, but the doors didn't unlock.

Muttering, he inserted the key into the door and unlocked it manually. Casting a quick glance into the fog to make sure the shadow wasn't lurking there, he slipped behind the wheel and put the keys in the ignition.

Nothing happened.

"Come on. Come on, you bastard! Please. Please start. Please?"

Dan tried again, pumping the gas pedal as he did. The results were the same. Then he tried putting the car on accessory and trying the radio. Like all of the other electronics, it was dead. His knuckles turned white as he gripped the wheel.

"Should have known better. Stupid, Dan. Real stupid. You're wasting time."

He got out of the car, pocketed the keys, and looked across the street again. After a moment's hesitation, he crossed over to the neighbor's house. The fog grew thick again, as if anticipating him. He paused at the edges of it. The mist swirled around his feet, lapping at his toes like surf. Dan cupped his hands over his mouth and took a deep breath.

"Hello? Can anybody hear me? Please, I need to know someone is there. I need to know I'm not... alone."

The word caught in his throat as that overpowering feeling of dread returned, a harbinger for the shadowy figure that appeared a moment later. The thing moved faster this time, closing the distance between them in only a few strides. It loomed over Dan, seeming to grow taller as it drew nearer. The mist parted before it, yet once again, Dan couldn't see the figure clearly. It remained a black, humanoid shadow, devoid of facial features or any other distinguishing characteristics. It reached for him without speaking, long arms outstretched, and this time, he was able to see the entity's hands. Like the rest of the figure, they were oversized. The shadow splayed its massive, elongated fingers. They were large enough to easily wrap themselves around Dan should the thing succeed in grasping him.

Dan felt rooted to the spot, as if he had stepped outside his body and was watching from above as the shadow reached for him. His mounting terror overrode every other sensation or thought. He couldn't speak or move. The mist churned and spun, swirling around them both. The temperature grew colder — the first thing he'd felt, other than his emotions, since getting out of bed.

Was this... *thing* responsible for everyone's disappearances, he wondered? Could it have attacked the neighborhood overnight, while he'd slept, abducting or murdering everyone else, but somehow missing him, until now? What was it? Alien? Supernatural? A figment of his imagination? Just a new addition to this unending nightmare from which he couldn't awaken?

The figure was directly overtop him now, and the fog encircled them, blocking out the rest of the world. Dan gaped, transfixed. Even this close, the entity still had no features. Its face was non-existent. There were no eyes or mouth or nose. It wore no clothing, that he could see, and had no genitalia, belly button, or anything else that would identify it as human. Its obsidian surface was marred only by tiny, swirling specks. Dan had to strain to see them. His first impression was of dust floating in a beam of sunlight, but he was certain that the specks weren't dust, and there was nothing light about his tormentor. Then all thought left him as the massive fingers brushed against his shoulders and waist.

"No!"

Turning, Dan ducked the creature's grasp and fled again. He barreled through the mist until his house reappeared. He cast one terrified glance over his shoulder. As before, the figure wasn't following him.

He ran into the house once more and slammed the door behind him. His hands were shaking and he fumbled with the lock. When he worked up the courage to peek out the window, he saw that the shadow was still there, lurking in the fog. It stood still as a statue, watching the house.

"What are you," Dan whispered. "What do you want?"

Eventually, the shadow turned and slowly vanished into the gray haze.

And then Dan was alone again.

6
____

With no electricity or even a working clock, it was hard for Dan to mark the passage of time. The murk outside didn't help matters. There was never a clear transition of daylight or darkness. There was only the oppressive gray half-light, as if the world were being lit by phosphorescent fungus. Neither the sun or the moon could be glimpsed through the fog, and the sky was empty of stars.

He was alone.

He sat. He tried to cry and couldn't. He sat some more. He sighed a lot. Occasionally, he attempted to eat something, not because he was hungry, but because it was something to fill the hours. Each time he tried, Dan ended up spitting the food out. All of it had that same flat, unpalatable, tasteless texture. He didn't shave. He didn't go to the bathroom. He didn't have to. His stubble didn't grow and his bladder and bowels remained quiet. And besides, with no plumbing or running water, he couldn't exactly bathe or wash up anyway. If he stank, he couldn't smell it. And so what if he did? It wasn't like there was anybody else around to complain. He didn't bother to change his clothes. The bathrobe and boxer shorts clung to him, but if they turned musty, he didn't notice.

He didn't sleep. He didn't need to. He didn't see the point. Why bother going to sleep when you already were? People never slept in their dreams, and he was most definitely dreaming, so fuck that noise.

And also, when he tried to sleep, he found that he couldn't. It was strange without Jerry next to him. He kept expecting to hear Jerry breathing or snoring, or to smell his cologne. Instead, there was nothing. The bed felt empty, as did the rest of the house. He felt like a stranger in his own home. He feared that if he closed his eyes, Danielle might return and he wouldn't see her. Or worse, the thing outside might decide to emerge from the mists again, and this time, it would come into the house. Even if he had felt sleepy, the thought of opening his eyes and finding that monstrosity looming over the bed was enough to keep him awake.

He tried to get drunk — and failed. Neither Dan or Jerry had been heavy drinkers, but they kept a stock on hand for when they had company. The bottles were stored on the top shelf of the kitchen cupboard, safe from Danielle's reach. Dan brought them all over to the kitchen table. He tried tequila, scotch, vodka, and beer. The liquors were tasteless, just like everything else, and the beer had gone flat. He forced himself to drink them anyway, but no matter how much he consumed, the effects were negligible.

He talked to himself. At first, it was just to break the silence and fill the void. Later, he'd catch himself in mid-sentence and realize he'd been doing it without knowing.

He laughed aloud.

Screamed aloud.

Tried to cry, and failed. The emotion was there. It was always there, threatening to rip him in half, but just like always, the tears themselves refused to flow.

He had no idea how long he went on that way. Two days. Maybe three? Perhaps four? Certainly no more than a week, though. In all that time, he did not know hunger or fatigue — only sadness and fear and an overwhelming sense of loneliness. The simple act of existing — of being alive — sent him into a fugue state of depression unlike anything he had ever known.

However little time had passed, it was enough. Eventually, the silence and monotony became unbearable, overshadowing even his fears of the shadow-being lurking outside. Dan convinced himself that the only way to end this nightmare was to embrace it. He tried to work up the nerve to walk outside and confront the entity head on.

"But what if I'm not dreaming?" he muttered. "What if that thing is real? What if I'm the only one left?"

He was still mulling this over when he heard a voice outside. It was a female voice, soft and faint, but noticeable simply because it was the only voice, other than his own, that he'd heard since Danielle's ghost... or vision... or whatever she'd been, had appeared to him.

"Hello," the voice called. "Is there anybody here?"

Dan bolted out of the chair, consumed with two thoughts. The first was that he recognized the voice. He was certain it belonged to Maria Lopez, the girl from next door. The second, more urgent thought was that Maria was in danger. If the shadow heard her calling, and got to her before he did...

...well, Dan still didn't know exactly what would happen, or what the entity's intentions were. But they certainly weren't good. How else to explain the terror that consumed him each time he encountered the thing?

"Hello?" Maria sounded closer to the house now. "What happens next? Is this it?"

Dan ran through the house and out the front door, sliding to a halt when he spotted Maria standing on the border between his yard and her parent's property. He stood there gaping, his robe hanging open, dimly aware of how he must look. Maria caught sight of him at the same time, and gasped. Her eyes went wide, and one pale hand fluttered to her mouth in surprise. That was when Dan noticed that something was wrong.

Two things, actually.

The first thing he noticed was that despite her normally dark complexion, Maria's arm was pale. The second thing he saw was that blood had streamed down her forearm, all the way to her elbow. The gray, false-light from the fog made the sight look even more garish than it already was. There was a cut in Maria's wrist, running from just beneath her palm to several inches down the underside of her forearm.

If you're going to do it right, Dan thought, *cut down, rather than across. Isn't that what they always used to say?*

He opened his mouth to speak, but all that came out was a sigh.

Maria said, "Holy shit!"

"Maria," Dan said. "Where did you come from? You're hurt!"

"Where did I come from? Shouldn't I be asking *you* that, Mr. Miller?"

He ignored her strange response, his attention focused instead on her obviously self-inflicted wound. He'd known the girl suffered from depression. Most of the neighbors knew, in fact. And she had supposedly threatened suicide a few times. But to be confronted with this serious attempt, was altogether unnerving. For a brief moment, Dan forgot all about his predicament, and his missing loved ones.

"You're hurt," he repeated. "Jesus Christ, Maria. We've got to get you some help!"

Laughing, she took a step backward. "It's a little late for that, don't you think?"

Dan noticed that the blood on her arm was dry. Instead of dripping, it had crusted like mud in the sun. When the girl took another step back, he saw that she'd cut both wrists, rather than just the one.

"Maria," he said softly, "what have you done?"

Instead of answering him, she glanced around the neighborhood and into the fog. "I don't get it. I thought there would be more than this. And I certainly didn't expect to see you here, Mr. Miller. I figured you were long gone."

"N-no," Dan stammered. "I've been here the whole time. I thought I was alone. I checked your house before. Nobody was home. Where are your parents? Have you seen anyone else? Have you seen Jerry or Danielle?"

She tilted her head to one side and frowned, staring at him.

"Mr. Miller... don't you—"

"Shhhhh! Quiet."

Dan felt it come over him as if someone had thrown a bucket of cold water at them — the terror, the dreadful certainty that the shadow-being was approaching. He glanced across the street and saw the mists churning. Seconds later, the haze parted and the figure strode toward them.

"Run," he shouted, rushing to her side. He grabbed Maria's injured arm without thinking, but she didn't cry out or wince. When she refused to move, he pulled her along behind him.

"Hey," Maria protested. "What the hell are you doing?"

"Don't you see it? Come on. We've got to get inside before it catches us. Hurry!"

"But Mr. Miller. What—"

"Now, Maria! Hurry up."

Despite her resistance, Dan dragged the teenager inside his house and slammed the door behind them. He locked it, and then crouched down on the floor, motioning for her to do the same. Frowning in confusion, she did as he asked. Dan put a finger to his lips, indicating for her to be quiet. Slowly, the fear subsided. After silently counting to one hundred, he crept to the window and peeked outside. The figure had retreated back into the mist, but it was still visible, lurking at the edge of the sidewalk, standing sentry over the house.

"Shit," he muttered. "Why won't it just go away? What does it want?"

"What is that thing?" Maria asked, crawling to his side.

"I don't know. I wish I did. It's fucking terrifying, whatever it is."

"Do you think so?"

Dan turned to her. "You mean to tell me you weren't scared of that thing?"

Maria shrugged. "No. Not really. Should I have been?"

Dan shook his head, unsure of how to respond. He turned back to the window. The entity hadn't moved. It was still there, watching.

"I don't think it will come inside," he said. "At least, it hasn't so far. I'm not sure why. I mean, given the size of that thing, there's no way I could stop it if it did decide to get inside, but for whatever reason, it doesn't. I think we're safe, for the moment. Let's go into the kitchen. I'll get the first aid kit from the bathroom and get you fixed up."

"But I don't need fixed up, Mr. Miller. I don't need—"

"Nonsense. Of course you do." He got up and walked toward the kitchen. "I'm not going to judge you, Maria. God knows I thought about it a few times when I was your age. I hadn't come out to my parents or my friends back then. The stress and pressure was... well, let's just say that there were times I thought that killing myself would be easier than being gay. But it's not worth it."

Pausing, he turned back to her. The girl stood at the window, her mouth open, staring.

"Come on," Dan said, trying to smile. "I'll get you taken care of and then we can talk about what's happened. Exchange notes. Because until now, I was sure that I must still be asleep. Thought I was dreaming. Maybe you did too?"

"We're not asleep, Mr. Miller."

Dan grinned. "Well, yeah. Obviously not. I know that now. But it still doesn't explain what happened or where everyone else has gone to. Have you seen anyone else?"

"No," she said. "I mean, I thought I might see somebody here, but I sure wasn't expecting you. No offense."

"None taken. Do you have any idea what it was or where they've gone? And really, Maria, we need to disinfect your arms and bandage them up before you get infected. Please?"

"My arms are fine!"

"Fine? You've cut them open, Maria!"

Her mouth went slack. She whistled, low and mournful, and then ran a hand through her hair.

"What?" Dan asked. "What's wrong?"

"You don't know, do you? I mean, you *really* don't know."

"Know? Know what? You mean what's happened? No, I don't know. Haven't you been listening?"

"Mr. Miller... Jesus. Maybe you'd better sit down."

"I'm fine," he insisted. "Now just tell me what's going on. Please?"

She took a deep breath. "You... I don't need you to fix my arms because I'm dead."

Dan stared at her. "What?"

"I'm dead, Mr. Miller. I killed myself just a few minutes ago."

"I—I don't understand. Dead?"

"It's a long story, and to be honest, I don't feel like talking about it. Suffice to say, there aren't a lot of people who will miss me. I wanted this. My parents were at work, and I got home from school, and I posted a goodbye message online, and then I did it. I used my father's box-cutter."

"But you're... that's... what?"

"I'm dead."

"Then how…? This doesn't make sense. If you're dead, then how are you here? How are we talking right now?"

"Because, Mr. Miller. Don't you see?"

Dan shook his head.

"Mr. Miller, you're dead, too."

"No, I'm not. I'm standing right here." Dan was aware of just how small and unsure he sounded.

"You're dead, Mr. Miller. You died over a year ago. You had a massive heart attack while you were asleep. Jerry discovered you the next morning when he woke up. He was really distraught."

"No. No, I'm sorry, but that's impossible. I'm not dead."

"Yeah, you are."

"No, I'm not!"

"I watched them carry you out myself. Danielle was crying, and Jerry was a mess. My parents and I watched her for him while he made all the arrangements."

"Stop it."

"I was at your funeral, Mr. Miller! You had an open casket and viewing. Trust me. You were dead."

"STOP IT! Why are you saying this? It's not true. It can't be true."

Her expression was sorrowful. "I'm sorry, but it is."

"You said I died over a year ago?"

She nodded. "Yes."

"Well, that right there proves it can't be true. I've only been here a few days. Not long at all. I haven't been eating or drinking, and I'm still the same weight I was, so it can't have been more than a few days."

Maria started to speak, but he interrupted.

"I want to know what's going on. The truth, this time. Where did you come from? I was just at your house a few days ago, and you weren't there then. Nobody was. I checked your place and the Kresby's. Hell, I broke their window, and nobody—"

"Wait a second! You broke the Kresby's window? You mean the big picture window at the front of their house?"

"Yes. That's the one. Why?"

"Holy shit." Maria leaned back against the wall and sighed. "I see what's happened now. I get it."

"Well, that makes one of us. I wish you'd explain it to me. And can we please go into the kitchen? I don't like standing here with that thing still hanging around outside. The living room feels too exposed."

Snickering, Maria stood up. "Okay."

"What's so funny?" Dan asked, as she joined him at the kitchen table.

"I'm sorry. Just the term. *Living* room. It struck me funny. Two dead people hanging out in the living room."

"I'm not dead, Maria. I really wish you'd stop saying that."

"Am I?" She held out her arms. "Look at me. Am I dead?"

"You're not bleeding anymore."

"That doesn't prove anything. Check my pulse, Mr. Miller."

"That wouldn't prove anything, either. I saw Danielle a few days ago. She was here one minute and gone the next. I don't know what she was — and I don't know what you are, either. But I'm not fucking dead."

Maria sighed again. Then she reached across the table and took his hand. Dan flinched, but didn't pull away. After being alone for so long, the physical contact eased his fears and worries. The girl certainly felt real enough.

"Mr. Miller, I'm going to ask you a few things. Things that there's no way I should know about. I just want you to answer me honestly, okay?"

Dan nodded.

"You said that you broke the Kresby's big picture window. Well, shortly after you passed away—"

"But I'm not dead."

"Just listen," she soothed. "Please?"

"Okay." Dan nodded. "Sorry. I'm just upset."

"That's okay. Anyway, shortly after you passed away, the Kresby's window was broken. It happened while they were watching TV. Nobody knew how it happened. The weather was nice. Sunny. No clouds or hail or anything like that. There weren't any kids running around outside or anything like that. It just... shattered."

"When I broke it," Dan said, "there was nobody inside the house. The television wasn't on. There's no electricity."

"Are you sure no one was home?"

"I... yes. Sort of. I thought I heard Susan scream, just for a second, but there was nobody there."

"A few months after that," Maria said, "Jerry told my Mom that he was afraid somebody had broken into your house. He called the cops and everything. Apparently, he woke up one morning and found ink stains all over his wallet. He also found some on Danielle's pillow. They were smudged, like finger-prints, but the cops were never able to get anything concrete from them. Do you know anything about that?"

Ink stains. Dan remembered the pen breaking in his grip, and how he'd smudged Jerry's wallet and Danielle's pillow when he was looking for them.

"Mr. Miller?"

He tried to speak, but there was a knot in his throat. Instead, he closed his eyes and nodded.

"A few months after that," Maria continued, "Danielle said she saw you. She broke down at school and they made Jerry come pick her up, and when she got home, she told him that she saw your ghost. It worried Jerry enough that he took her to see a child counselor. But the counselor said it was just her dealing with her grief and expressing it through a fantasy outlet, and it didn't happen again."

"I saw her," Dan whispered. "Upstairs, in her room. I saw Danielle. She was a ghost."

"No," Maria said. "She wasn't the ghost. You were."

"But... but that's... how?"

"I don't know. You died in your sleep a little over a year ago, Mr. Miller. Don't you remember anything about what happened?"

"I went to sleep. When I woke up, Jerry and Danielle were gone. The house was empty. The power and the utilities were off. And everything... everything tasted funny. Even the sound seemed off. Not off like the power, but different. You know what I mean?"

"I've noticed the sound is different here," Maria agreed.

"But where is here? Where are we? We're in my house. Everything looks the same. This isn't Heaven or Hell. Not that I believe in those anyway."

"I don't know," Maria said. "Maybe this is where you remained. Maybe you created it. Or maybe we see our homes when we die. Our immediate worlds. Because after I cut my wrists, I remember getting very cold and very sleepy. When I woke up, I was dead, but still in my room. When I came outside, I saw you. How far have you explored over the last year?"

"It hasn't been a year," Dan insisted. "I'm telling you, I've only been here for a few days."

"Maybe time is different here? Maybe what only felt like a few days here, was a lot longer back where we... well, you know."

"There's nothing out there," Dan said. "Nothing beyond the mist."

"Did you go into it?"

He nodded. "A little bit. But there's nothing there."

"Maybe our memories only keep our immediate surroundings in place. Maybe everything else vanishes."

"Well then, what about that thing out there? What the hell is it?"

"I don't know," Maria said, "but I do know that I wasn't afraid of it. I don't think it meant us any harm. I felt very calm when it came toward us."

"Calm? Jesus Christ, I was terrified of it."

"Do you know why?"

"No. Do you?"

"No," Maria admitted. "Maybe it's because you didn't realize you were dead."

"But what does it want? What is it?"

"Maybe it's here to help us. To guide us somehow."

"How can you know for sure?"

Maria shrugged. "I don't. But I feel things. In the last few minutes, ever since waking up after I died—I feel things that are true. Things I didn't know before."

"I don't understand."

"I'm not sure I do, either. But I feel them anyway. I bet you can, too."

"All I felt was scared. There were no universal truths revealed to me. All this time, all that I've felt is alone."

"Maybe you weren't ready yet. After all, you didn't know what you were until now."

"I still don't! How can I be dead? How can—"

Dan was interrupted by a knock at the door. Unlike the rest of the sounds, the knock was deep and loud. Two more followed, each one powerful and insistent.

"Oh God," Dan moaned. "It's the shadow. I know it is."

"It's okay," Maria said. "You don't have to be afraid of it. Stop for a moment and think about it. Let yourself feel."

Dan took a deep breath and did as she asked. He was surprised to discover that Maria was right. That sense of foreboding that had come over him every time the shadow drew near was now gone. Instead, he felt a strange sense of comfort and peace.

"What do we do now?" he whispered.

Maria stood up and smiling, took his hand. "Let's open the door."

They did, and the figure was there to greet them. It made a sweeping gesture with one large hand, indicating the direction they should go. Maria stepped forward eagerly. After a moment's hesitation, Dan followed. The shadow walked between them, and when it took their hands in its own, Dan was no longer afraid.

Around them, the mists dissipated and the gray turned into light. The skies above burned with dark shades of orange and red and yellow, and the light grew brighter, illuminating them.

"Where are we going?" Dan asked. "Where is it taking us?"

"To the next place."

"And where is that?"

Maria smiled. "Let's find out together, Mr. Miller."

Dan shielded his eyes with his free hand as the dazzling light consumed them, enfolding them in its radiance.

And then, he was no longer alone.

AFTERWORD

Spoiler Warning: If you are one of those people who skip to the end of the book before you read the story, stop now. The following anecdote contains major spoilers and will ruin your enjoyment of this novella.

Seriously. Stop reading. Go back to the beginning of the book.

I mean it. Get the hell out of here.

Okay, are they gone?

Good. Now, where was I? Oh, yes. Alone.

Alone has been sitting inside my head for over a decade now. The idea came from a conversation I had with my dear friend, noted critic and genre scholar Jack Haringa, many years ago at some long-forgotten horror convention. We were discussing Fredric Brown's infamous short story, "Knock". If you're not familiar with the tale, "Knock" was quite famous in its time for being the shortest science fiction story ever written. The original version went like this:

The last man on earth sat in his room.
There was a knock at the door.

That's it. Two sentences. Short and sweet, and packing one hell of a punch. But then, at the urging of his peers, Brown continued the story, elaborating on those first two sentences. He further developed the plot and the character. The last man turned out to be named Walter Phelan, and the entity knocking on his door was an alien known as Zan, who had killed off everyone else on Earth and wanted to put Walter in a cosmic zoo (along with the planet's last woman, Grace).

I told Jack that I thought the story would have worked better had the author just stuck to those first two sentences, because I thought the whole alien zoo thing was silly. I thought it was silly because I'd seen it done in the Marvel and DC comic books of my youth, and I was young enough, stupid enough, and conceited enough not to understand that those Marvel and DC Comics were simply riffing on Brown, who had done it first. (I know better now, because I am old).

Jack asked me what I would have done differently, were I to continue the story from those first two lines. Before I could answer him, we were interrupted by Jack Ketchum, who had a bottle of Dewar's whiskey that he needed help drinking, and then both Jacks got very drunk and began hollering at me about my incorrect usage of the semi-colon (which many people do, and not always when they are drunk), and I never did get the chance to tell Jack Haringa what I would have done differently with the story.

So I wrote this instead. *Alone* is what I would have done differently.

I still think Brown would have been better off sticking with just the original two sentences. Although I do not know for certain, I would hazard a guess that he found expanding upon them to be a challenge. I know that I sure did. *Alone* wasn't an easy novella to write. Once I got past the initial plot — Dan wakes up alone and finds out that he's the last man on Earth — it was hard to balance the discovery portions of the plot in a way that a) wouldn't give away the fact that he's dead and b) wouldn't drag the story down to a tedious snail's pace. It was extremely difficult to juggle the plot and sustain the narrative in a way that served both the story and the reader.

An aside: when *The Sixth Sense* was first released to movie theaters, authors Rain Graves and Geoff Cooper went to see it together. Ten minutes into the movie, Coop turned toward Rainy and said, "Bruce Willis is a ghost. I'm going outside to smoke. See you when the movie is done." With *Alone*, the main thing I wanted to avoid was you, the reader, having the same realization with this novella that Coop had with the film. Hopefully, I succeeded. If not... well, I did my best. That's all any writer can do.

An early draft of *Alone*, written several years ago, introduced the Grim Reaper as a character during the second chapter. I scrapped that version, and in hindsight, I'm glad I did. It was the work of a younger writer who wanted to rush ahead and get to the spot where he could shout, "Boo! I got you readers! Dan is a ghost! He's been dead this whole time! M. Night Shyamalan's got nothing on me." Maria appeared much earlier in that draft, as well, and much of the novella involved her and Dan trying to escape the Reaper, who was very angry that they were refusing to move on to the next level of existence.

I like this quiet, stripped down, acoustic version better. I hope you did, too.

Brian Keene
April 2011

ABOUT THE AUTHOR

Brian Keene is the author of over fifty books, mostly in the horror, crime, and fantasy genres. He has also written for such media properties as *Thor, Doom Patrol, Justice League, Doctor Who, The X-Files, Aliens,* and *Masters of the Universe*. Several of his novels and stories have been adapted for film.

His numerous awards and honors include the 2014 World Horror Grandmaster Award, 2001 Bram Stoker Award for Nonfiction, 2003 Bram Stoker Award for First Novel, the 2016 Imadjinn Award for Best Fantasy Novel, and the 2015 Imaginarium Film Festival Awards for Best Screenplay, Best Short Film Genre, and Best Short Film Overall.

Keene also serves on the Board of Directors for the Scares That Care 501c charity organization.

He lives in rural Pennsylvania, along the banks of the Susquehanna River, with his wife (author Mary Sangiovanni), and their five cats, thirteen hermit crabs, and assorted deer, possums, raccoons, bears, eagles, and other wildlife.